MW00764717

I'm Just a Little Someone

To: Jenna

In Friendship Kindness and Gratitude

Sharen S. Peters
:) ♡

Written by
Sharen S. Peters

Illustrated by
Amanda Alter

LifeLong Friends Publishers, LLC

Mansfield Center, CT

Copyright © 2017   Sharen S. Peters

All Rights Reserved.

No part of this publication may be reproduced, stored in a retrieval system or transmitted, in any form or by any means—electronic, mechanical, photocopying, recording or otherwise—without prior written permission from the publisher, except for the inclusion of brief quotations in a review.

LifeLong Friends Publishers, LLC
P.O. Box 483
Mansfield Center, CT 06250
www.LifeLongFriends.com

ISBN 978-0-9971221-0-7   printed book
ISBN 978-0-9971221-1-4   ebook

Cover and interior design: Anita Jones, AnotherJones.com
Illustrations: Amanda Alter

Publisher's Cataloging-In-Publication Data
(Prepared by The Donohue Group, Inc.)

Names: Peters, Sharen S. | Alter, Amanda, illustrator.
Title: I'm just a little someone / written by Sharen S. Peters ; illustrated by Amanda Alter.
Other Titles: I am just a little someone
Description: Mansfield Center, CT : LifeLong Friends Publishers, LLC [2017] | Series: [Friends for Life series] ; [1] | Interest age level: 003-006. | Includes activities. | Summary: "A lonely little girl doll sees a little boy doll across the room in a toy store. He looks lonely too. She invites him over to sit on her shelf. They play with her toys, read books and talk together. They are both laughing and giggling when they see another little someone who also looks lonely. This time it is a four legged animal with the biggest brown eyes. He jumps up to her shelf and then the three of them are as happy as can be! Together they become best friends."--Provided by publisher.
Identifiers: ISBN 978-0-9971221-0-7 (print) | ISBN 978-0-9971221-1-4 (ebook)
Subjects: LCSH: Friendship--Juvenile fiction. | Loneliness--Juvenile fiction. | Dolls--Juvenile fiction. | Stuffed animals (Toys)--Juvenile fiction. | CYAC: Friendship--Fiction. | Loneliness--Fiction. | Dolls--Fiction. | Stuffed animals (Toys)--Fiction.
Classification: LCC PZ7.1.P48 Im 2017 (print) | LCC PZ7.1.P4 (ebook) | DDC [E]--dc23

Printed in The United States of America

I'm just a little someone
Sitting on a shelf

I'm just a little someone
As lonely as can be

All the people
walking by
But no one looks
at me.

And then one day across the room
Upon another shelf
I see another someone
Alone all by himself

"Come on over
And sit with me!"

It was then I saw
His big wide smile

As he came
to my shelf
To sit for
a while.

We giggled and laughed
With the girls and boys

And watched
them play
With all
our toys.

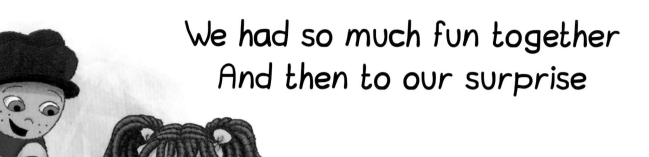

We had so much fun together
And then to our surprise

Another little someone
Caught our very eyes.

He had four paws
And with one
big jump

He was on our shelf
Rolled up in a lump.

And now it's just the three of us
Upon my little shelf

Happy as three friends can be
No longer by myself

Activities

1. This story takes place in a toy store. Look at pages 6, 7, 15, and 17. There are lots of colored blocks. Pick your favorite page and count the blocks. Remember to include the numbered blocks on the bottom of the page.

2. Name the numbers and colors on blocks on the bottom of the same page.

3. Look on page 19. What are the colors on the boy doll's clothing? What are the colors on the girl doll's clothing?

4. Look on page 7. Count all the blue books. Now count all the red books.

5. Look on page 18. See the girl and boy laughing. What are they doing?

6. What do you like to do for fun with your friends? Draw a picture of you having fun with your friends.

7. Who is your special friend? Friends can be animals, toys, dolls, stuffed animals or anyone or anything that makes you happy.

8. Look on page 9. See the sad face of the boy doll. Now, look on page 1. See the sad face of the girl doll. Why are they so sad?

9. Look on page 17. Look at the boy doll and girl doll on the shelf. Why are they giggling and laughing? Are they happy? Do you know why?

10. Draw two circles on a piece of paper. Draw a sad face on one circle and a happy face on the second circle.

11. Teachers, parents, home school parents, therapists...you can prepare plain paper plates for heads. Die-cut or pre-cut circles for eyes...half-moons for smiles or frowns to paste on the plates to show emotions of the boy and girl dolls or characters in the story...yarn and other craft items can be used to decorate the faces with hair, freckles, etc.

12. Look on page 7. See the two boys on the floor. What are they doing? How are they helping each other?

13. *Look on page 9. Look at the boy in green. What does he have in his hand? Can you tell who owns the hat? He is playing with the little boy in yellow with his hat. They are laughing and having fun.*

14. *Look on pages 16 and 17. What happened? Now the boy in yellow is playing with the boy in green with his hat on the helicopter! What is he doing?*

15. *Look on page 15. What is the girl doll doing? Draw a picture of you helping a friend.*

16. *Are you nice to your friends? Are your friends nice to you? Draw a picture of how you feel when your friends are nice to you. Draw a picture of how you feel when your friends are not nice to you.*

17. *Draw a picture of a sad face and show it to the girl or boy sitting next to you. If a person is sad, what can you do to make them feel better?*

18. *Look on page 21. Do you see a little dog? Look on page 22. What is the dog doing?*

19. *What did you like about the story?*

About the Author

As a way of coping with sadness and loneliness in her childhood, author Sharen S. Peters began writing poetry in her teenage years. She has been writing ever since but just recently has begun to share her words in hopes it will help other lonely children. Sharen graduated with an MBA from the University of Connecticut and has a Dental Hygiene Certificate from the University of Pennsylvania. She resides in New England with her husband Tom. Their 15-year-old sheltie, Rebel, has become a part of their family story.

About the Illustrator

Amanda Alter is an illustrator and graphic designer from Connecticut. Her passion for art goes back to childhood, when she would be caught doodling in every class. She received her BA in Graphic Design plus additional fine arts course work from Southern Connecticut State University. Children's book illustration is her true passion, but she enjoys multiple genres of art and design.

Sharen was a lonely child in her early years, keeping to herself but longing for close friends. Writing was a way to capture her feelings and create a life of connection with others. While in graduate school at the University of Connecticut she met her husband Tom. Life became shared with happy times and the fulfillment she had only written about. They adopted a sheltie, Rebel, in 2001 who became their 'canine son.' Now, as a family of three, Sharen shares her writings of her earlier life with full illustrations for children, giving messages of hope, encouragement, and friendship.

Watch for more books coming in the ***Friends for Life Series***
www.LifeLongFriends.com